A. V. Laider

Max Beerbohm

Contents

A. V. LAIDER

BY

Max Beerbohm

A. V. Laider By MAX BEERBOHM

I unpacked my things and went down to await luncheon.

It was good to be here again in this little old sleepy hostel by the sea. Hostel I say, though it spelt itself without an "s" and even placed a circumflex above the "o." It made no other pretension. It was very cozy indeed.

I had been here just a year before, in mid-February, after an attack of influenza. And now I had returned, after an attack of influenza. Nothing was changed. It had been raining when I left, and the waiter--there was but a single, a very old waiter-- had told me it was only a shower. That waiter was still here, not a day older. And the shower had not ceased.

Steadfastly it fell on to the sands, steadfastly into the iron-gray sea. I stood look- ing out at it from the windows of the hall, admiring it very much. There seemed to be little else to do. What little there was I did. I mastered the contents of a blue hand-bill which, pinned to the wall just beneath the framed engraving of Queen Victoria's Coronation, gave token of a concert that was to be held--or, rather, was to have been held some weeks ago--in the town hall for the benefit of the Life-Boat Fund. I looked at the barometer, tapped it, was not the wiser. I wandered to the letter-board.

These letter-boards always fascinate me. Usually some two or three of the en- velops stuck into the cross-garterings have a certain newness and freshness. They seem sure they will yet be claimed. Why not? Why SHOULDN'T John Doe, Esq., or Mrs. Richard Roe turn up at any moment? I do not know. I can only say that nothing in the world seems to me more unlikely. Thus it is that these young bright envelops touch my heart even more than do their dusty and sallowed seniors. Sour resignation is less touching than impatience for what will not be, than the eagerness that has to wane and wither. Soured beyond measure these old envelops are. They are not nearly so nice as they should be to the young ones. They lose no chance of sneering and discouraging. Such dialogues as this are only too frequent:

A Very Young Envelop: Something in me whispers that he will come to-day!

A Very Old Envelop: He? Well, that's good! Ha, ha, ha! Why didn't he come last week, when YOU came? What reason have you for supposing he'll ever come now? It isn't as if he were a frequenter of the place. He's never been here. His name is utterly unknown here. You don't suppose he's coming on the chance of finding YOU?

A. V. Y. E.: It may seem silly, but--something in me whispers--

A. V. O. E.: Something in YOU? One has only to look at you to see there's nothing in you but a note scribbled to him by a cousin. Look at ME! There are three sheets, closely written, in ME. The lady to whom I am addressed--

A. V. Y. E.: Yes, sir, yes; you told me all about her yesterday.

A. V. O. E.: And I shall do so to-day and to-morrow and every day and all day long. That young lady was a widow. She stayed here many times. She was delicate, and the air suited her. She was poor, and the tariff was just within her means. She was lonely, and had need of love. I have in me for her a passionate avowal and strictly honorable proposal, written to her, after many rough copies, by a gentleman who had made her acquaintance under this very roof. He was rich, he was charming, he was in the prime of life. He had asked if he might write to her. She had flutteringly granted his request. He posted me to her the day after his return to London. I looked forward to being torn open by her. I was very sure she would wear me and my contents next to her bosom. She was gone. She had left no address. She never returned. This I tell you, and shall continue to tell you, not because I want any of your callow sympathy,--no, THANK you!--but that you may judge how much less than slight are the probabilities that you yourself--

But my reader has overheard these dialogues as often as I. He wants to know what was odd about this particular letter-board before which I was standing. At first glance I saw nothing odd about it. But presently I distinguished a handwriting that was vaguely familiar. It was mine. I stared, I wondered. There is always a slight shock in seeing an envelop of one's own after it has gone through the post. It looks as if it had gone through so much. But this was the first time I had ever seen an envelop of mine eating its heart out in bondage on a letter-board. This was outrageous. This was hardly to be believed. Sheer kindness had impelled me to write to "A. V. Laider, Esq.," and this was the result! I hadn't minded receiving no answer. Only now, indeed, did I remember that I hadn't received one. In multitudinous London the memory of A. V. Laider and his trouble had soon passed from my mind. But--well, what a lesson not to go out of one's way to write to casual acquaintances!

My envelop seemed not to recognize me as its writer. Its gaze was the more piteous for being blank. Even so had I once been gazed at by a dog that I had lost and, after many days, found in the Battersea Home. "I don't know who you are, but, whoever you are, claim me, take me out of this!" That was my dog's appeal. This was the appeal of my envelop.

I raised my hand to the letter-board, meaning to effect a swift and lawless rescue, but paused at sound of a footstep behind me. The old waiter had come to tell me that my luncheon was ready. I followed him out of the hall, not, however, without a bright glance across my shoulder to reassure the little captive that I should come back.

I had the sharp appetite of the convalescent, and this the sea air had whetted already to a finer edge. In touch with a dozen oysters, and with stout, I soon shed away the unreasoning anger I had felt against A. V. Laider. I became merely sorry for him that he had not received a letter which might perhaps have comforted him. In touch with cutlets, I felt how sorely he had needed comfort. And anon, by the big bright fireside of that small dark smoking-room where, a year ago, on the last evening of my stay here, he and I had at length spoken to each other, I reviewed in detail the tragic experience he had told me; and I simply reveled in reminiscent sympathy with him.

A. V. LAIDER--I had looked him up in the visitors'-book on the night of his arrival. I myself had arrived the day before, and had been rather sorry there was no one else staying here. A convalescent by the sea likes to have some one to observe, to wonder about, at meal-time. I was glad when, on my second evening, I found seated at the table opposite to mine another guest. I was the gladder because he was just the right kind of guest. He was enigmatic. By this I mean that he did not look soldierly or financial or artistic or anything definite at all. He offered a clean slate for speculation. And, thank heaven! he evidently wasn't going to spoil the fun by engaging me in conversation later on. A decently unsociable man, anxious to be left alone.

The heartiness of his appetite, in contrast with his extreme fragility of aspect and limpness of demeanor, assured me that he, too, had just had influenza. I liked him for that. Now and again our eyes met and were instantly parted. We managed, as a rule, to observe each other indirectly. I was sure it was not merely because he had been ill that he looked interesting. Nor did it seem to me that a spiritual melancholy, though I imagined him sad at the best of times, was his sole asset. I conjectured that he was clever. I thought he might also be imaginative. At first glance I had mistrusted him. A shock of white hair, combined with a young face and dark eyebrows, does somehow make a man look like a charlatan. But it is foolish to be guided by an accident of color. I had soon rejected my first impression of my fellow-diner. I found him very sympathetic.

Anywhere but in England it would be impossible for two solitary men, howsoever much reduced by influenza, to spend five or six days in the same hostel and not exchange a single word. That is one of the charms of England. Had Laider and I been born and bred in any other land than Eng we should have become acquainted before the end of our first evening in the small smoking-room, and have found ourselves irrevocably committed to go on talking to each other throughout the rest of our visit. We might, it is true, have happened to like each other more than any one we had ever met. This off chance may have occurred to us both. But it counted for nothing against the certain surrender of quietude and liberty. We slightly bowed to each other as we entered or left the dining-room or smoking-room, and as we met on the wide-spread sands or in the shop that had a small and faded circulating library. That was all. Our mutual aloofness was a positive bond between us.

Had he been much older than I, the responsibility for our silence would of course have been his alone. But he was not, I judged, more than five or six years ahead of me, and thus I might without impropriety have taken it on myself to perform that hard and perilous feat which English people call, with a shiver, "breaking the ice." He had reason, therefore, to be as grateful to me as I to him. Each of us, not the less frankly because silently, recognized his obligation to the other. And when, on the last evening of my stay, the ice actually was broken there was no illwill between us: neither of us was to blame.

It was a Sunday evening. I had been out for a long last walk and had come in very late to dinner. Laider had left his table almost directly after I sat down to mine. When I entered the smoking-room I found him reading a weekly review which I had bought the day before. It was a crisis. He could not silently offer nor could I have silently accepted, six-pence. It was a crisis. We faced it like men. He made, by word of mouth, a graceful apology. Verbally, not by signs, I besought him to go on reading. But this, of course, was a vain counsel of perfection. The social code forced us to talk now. We obeyed it like men. To reassure him that our position was not so desperate as it might seem, I took the earliest opportunity to mention that I was going away early next morning. In the tone of his "Oh, are you?" he tried bravely to imply that he was sorry, even now, to hear that. In a way, perhaps, he really was sorry. We had got on so well together, he and I. Nothing could efface the memory of that. Nay, we seemed to be hitting it off even now. Influenza was not our sole theme. We passed from that to the aforesaid weekly review, and to a correspondence that was raging therein on faith and reason.

This correspondence had now reached its fourth and penultimate stage--its Australian stage. It is hard to see why these correspondences spring up; one only knows that they do spring up, suddenly, like street crowds. There comes, it would seem, a moment when the whole English-speaking race is unconsciously bursting to have its say about some one thing--the split infinitive, or the habits of migratory birds, or faith and reason, or what-not. Whatever weekly review happens at such a moment to contain a reference, however remote, to the theme in question reaps the storm. Gusts of letters come in from all corners of the British Isles. These are presently reinforced by Canada in full blast. A few weeks later the Anglo-Indians weigh in. In due course we have the help of our Australian cousins. By that time, however, we of the mother country have got our second wind, and so determined are we to make the most of it that at last even the editor suddenly loses patience and says, "This correspondence must now cease.--Ed." and wonders why on earth he ever allowed anything so tedious and idiotic to begin.

I pointed out to Laider one of the Australian letters that had especially pleased me in the current issue. It was from "A Melbourne Man," and was of the abrupt kind which declares that "all your correspondents have been groping in the dark" and then settles the whole matter in one short sharp flash. The flash in this instance was "Reason is faith, faith reason--that is all we know on earth and all we need to know." The writer then inclosed his card and was, etc., "A Melbourne Man." I said to Laider how very restful it was, after influenza, to read anything that meant nothing whatsoever. Laider was inclined to take the letter more seriously than I, and to be mildly metaphysical. I said that for me faith and reason were two separate things, and as I am no good at metaphysics, however mild, I offered a definite example, to coax the talk on to ground where I should be safer.

"Palmistry, for example," I said. "Deep down in my heart I believe in palmistry."

Laider turned in his chair.

"You believe in palmistry?"

I hesitated.

"Yes, somehow I do. Why? I haven't the slightest notion. I can give myself all sorts of reasons for laughing it to scorn. My common sense utterly rejects it. Of course the shape of the hand means something, is more or less an index of character. But the idea that my past and future are neatly mapped out on my palms--" I shrugged my shoulders.

"You don't like that idea?" asked Laider in his gentle, rather academic voice.

"I only say it's a grotesque idea."

"Yet you do believe in it?"

"I've a grotesque belief in it, yes."

"Are you sure your reason for calling this idea 'grotesque' isn't merely that you dislike it?"

"Well," I said, with the thrilling hope that he was a companion in absurdity, "doesn't it seem grotesque to you?"

"It seems strange."

"You believe in it?"

"Oh, absolutely."

"Hurrah!"

He smiled at my pleasure, and I, at the risk of reentanglement in metaphysics, claimed him as standing shoulder to shoulder with me against "A Melbourne Man." This claim he gently disputed.

"You may think me very prosaic," he said, "but I can't believe without evidence."

"Well, I'm equally prosaic and equally at a disadvantage: I can't take my own belief as evidence, and I've no other evidence to go on."

He asked me if I had ever made a study of palmistry. I said I had read one of Desbarolles's books years ago, and one of Heron-Allen's. But, he asked, had I tried to test them by the lines on my own hands or on the hands of my friends? I confessed that my actual practice in palmistry had been of a merely passive kind--the prompt extension of my palm to any one who would be so good as to "read" it and truckle for a few minutes to my egoism. (I hoped Laider might do this.)

"Then I almost wonder," he said, with his sad smile, "that you haven't lost your belief, after all the nonsense you must have heard. There are so many young girls who go in for palmistry. I am sure all the five foolish virgins were 'awfully keen on it' and used to say, 'You can be led, but not driven,' and, 'You are likely to have a serious illness between the ages of forty and forty-five,' and, 'You are by nature rather lazy, but can be very energetic by fits and starts.' And most of the professionals, I'm told, are as silly as the young girls."

For the honor of the profession, I named three practitioners whom I had found really good at reading character. He asked whether any of them had been right about past events. I confessed that, as a matter of fact, all three of them had been right in the main. This seemed to amuse him. He asked whether any of them had predicted anything which had since come true. I confessed that all three had predicted that I should do several things which I had since done rather unexpectedly. He asked if I didn't accept this as, at any rate, a scrap of evidence. I said I could only regard it as a fluke--a rather remarkable fluke.

The superiority of his sad smile was beginning to get on my nerves. I wanted him to see that he was as absurd as I.

"Suppose," I said--"suppose, for the sake of argument, that you and I are nothing but helpless automata created to do just this and that, and to have just that and this done to us. Suppose, in fact, we HAVEN'T any free will whatsoever. Is it likely or conceivable that the Power which fashioned us would take the trouble to jot down in cipher on our hands just what was in store for us?"

Laider did not answer this question; he did but annoyingly ask me another.

"You believe in free will?"

"Yes, of course. I'll be hanged if I'm an automaton."

"And you believe in free will just as in palmistry--without any reason?"

"Oh, no. Everything points to our having free will."

"Everything? What, for instance?"

This rather cornered me. I dodged out, as lightly as I could, by saying:

"I suppose YOU would say it's written in my hand that I should be a believer in free will."

"Ah, I've no doubt it is."

I held out my palms. But, to my great disappointment, he looked quickly away from them. He had ceased to smile. There was agitation in his voice as he explained that he never looked at people's hands now. "Never now--never again." He shook his head as though to beat off some memory.

I was much embarrassed by my indiscretion. I hastened to tide over the awkward moment by saying that if _I_ could read hands I wouldn't, for fear of the awful things I might see there.

"Awful things, yes," he whispered, nodding at the fire.

"Not," I said in self-defense, "that there's anything very awful, so far as I know, to be read in MY hands."

He turned his gaze from the fire to me.

"You aren't a murderer, for example?"

"Oh, no," I replied, with a nervous laugh.

"_I_ am."

This was a more than awkward, it was a painful, moment for me; and I am afraid I must have started or winced, for he instantly begged my pardon.

"I don't know," he exclaimed, "why I said it. I'm usually a very reticent man. But sometimes--" He pressed his brow. "What you must think of me!"

I begged him to dismiss the matter from his mind.

"It's very good of you to say that; but--I've placed myself as well as you in a false position. I ask you to believe that I'm not the sort of man who is 'wanted' or ever was 'wanted' by the police. I should be bowed out of any police-station at which I gave myself up. I'm not a murderer in any bald sense of the word. No."

My face must have perceptibly brightened, for, "Ah," he said, "don't imagine I'm not a murderer at all. Morally, I am." He looked at the clock. I pointed out that the night was young. He assured me that his story was not a long one. I assured him that I hoped it was. He said I was very kind. I denied this. He warned me that what he had to tell might rather tend to stiffen my unwilling faith in palmistry, and to shake my opposite and cherished faith in free will. I said, "Never mind." He stretched his hands pensively toward the fire. I settled myself back in my chair.

"My hands," he said, staring at the backs of them, "are the hands of a very weak man. I dare say you know enough of palmistry to see that for yourself. You notice the slightness of the thumbs and of he two 'little' fingers. They are the hands of a weak and over-sensitive man--a man without confidence, a man who would certainly waver in an emergency. Rather Hamletish hands," he mused. "And I'm like Hamlet in other respects, too: I'm no fool, and I've rather a noble disposition, and I'm unlucky. But Hamlet was luckier than I in one thing: he was a murderer by accident, whereas the murders that I committed one day fourteen years ago--for I must tell you it wasn't one murder, but many murders that I committed--were all of them due to the wretched inherent weakness of my own wretched self.

"I was twenty-six--no, twenty-seven years old, and rather a nondescript person, as I am now. I was supposed to have been called to the bar. In fact, I believe I HAD been called to the bar. I hadn't listened to the call. I never intended to practise, and I never did practise. I only wanted an excuse in the eyes of the world for existing. I suppose the nearest I have ever come to practicing is now at this moment: I am defending a murderer. My father had left me well enough provided with money. I was able to go my own desultory way, riding my hobbies where I would. I had a good stableful of hobbies. Palmistry was one of them. I was rather ashamed of this one. It seemed to me absurd, as it seems to you. Like you, though, I believed in it. Unlike you, I had done more than merely read a book about it. I had read innumerable books about it. I had taken casts of all my friends' hands. I had tested and tested again the points at which Desbarolles dissented from the Gipsies, and--well, enough that I had gone into it all rather thoroughly, and was as sound a palmist, as a man may be without giving his whole life to palmistry.

"One of the first things I had seen in my own hand, as soon as I had learned to read it, was that at about the age of twenty-six I should have a narrow escape from death--from a violent death. There was a clean break in the life-line, and a square joining it--the protective square, you know. The markings were precisely the same in both hands. It was to be the narrowest escape possible. And I wasn't going to escape without injury, either. That is what bothered me. There was a faint line connecting the break in the lifeline with a star on the line of health. Against that star was another square. I was to recover from the injury, whatever it might be. Still, I didn't exactly look forward to it. Soon after I had reached the age of twenty-five, I began to feel uncomfortable. The thing might be going to happen at any moment. In palmistry, you know, it is impossible to pin an event down hard and fast to one year. This particular event was to be when I was ABOUT twenty-six; it mightn't be till I was twenty-seven; it might be while I was only twenty-five.

"And I used to tell myself it mightn't be at all. My reason rebelled against the whole notion of palmistry, just as yours does. I despised my faith in the thing, just as you despise yours. I used to try not to be so ridiculously careful as I was whenever I crossed a street. I lived in London at that time. Motor-cars had not yet come in, but--what hours, all told, I must have spent standing on curbs, very circumspect, very lamentable! It was a pity, I suppose, that I had no definite occupation--something to take me out of myself. I was one of the victims of private means. There came a time when I drove in four-wheelers rather than in hansoms, and was doubtful of four-wheelers. Oh, I assure you, I was very lamentable indeed.

"If a railway-journey could be avoided, I avoided it. My uncle had a place in Hampshire. I was very fond of him and of his wife. Theirs was the only house I ever went to stay in now. I was there for a week in November, not long after my twenty-seventh birthday. There were other people staying there, and at the end of the week we all traveled back to London together. There were six of us in the carriage: Colonel Elbourn and his wife and their daughter, a girl of seventeen; and another married couple, the Bretts. I had been at Winchester with Brett, but had hardly seen him since that time. He was in the Indian Civil, and was home on leave. He was sailing for India next week. His wife was to remain in England for some months, and then join him out there. They had been married five years. She was now just twenty-four years old. He told me that this was her age. The Elbourns I had never met before. They were charming people. We had all been very happy together. The only trouble had been that on the last night, at dinner, my uncle asked me if I still went in for 'the Gipsy business,' as he always called it; and of course the three ladies were immensely excited, and implored me to 'do' their hands. I told them it was all nonsense, I said I had forgotten all I once knew, I made various excuses; and the matter dropped. It was quite true that I had given up reading hands. I avoided anything that might remind me of what was in my own hands. And so, next morning, it was a great bore to me when, soon after the train started, Mrs. Elbourn said it would be 'too cruel' of me if I refused to do their hands now. Her daughter and Mrs. Brett also said it would be 'brutal'; and they were all taking off their gloves, and--well, of course I had to give in.

"I went to work methodically on Mrs. Elbourn's hands, in the usual way, you know, first sketching the character from the backs of them; and there was the usual hush, broken by the usual little noises--grunts of assent from the husband, cooings of recognition from the daughter. Presently I asked to see the palms, and from them I filled in the details of Mrs. Elbourn's character before going on to the events in her life. But while I talked I was calculating how old Mrs. Elbourn might be. In my first glance at her palms I had seen that she could not have been less than twenty-five when she married. The daughter was seventeen. Suppose the daughter had been born a year later--how old would the mother be? Forty-three, yes. Not less than that, poor woman!"

Laider looked at me.

"Why 'poor woman!' you wonder? Well, in that first glance I had seen other things than her marriage-line. I had seen a very complete break in the lines of life and of fate. I had seen violent death there. At what age? Not later, not possibly LATER, than forty-three. While I talked to her about the things that had happened in her girlhood, the back of my brain was hard at work on those marks of catastrophe. I was horribly wondering that she was still alive. It was impossible that between her and that catastrophe there could be more than a few short months. And all the time I was talking; and I suppose I acquitted myself well, for I remember that when I ceased I had a sort of ovation from the Elbourns.

"It was a relief to turn to another pair of hands. Mrs. Brett was an amusing young creature, and her hands were very characteristic, and prettily odd in form. I allowed myself to be rather whimsical about her nature, and having begun in that vein, I went on in it, somehow, even after she had turned her palms. In those palms were reduplicated the signs I had seen in Mrs. Elbourn's. It was as though they had been copied neatly out. The only difference was in the placing of them; and it was this difference that was the most horrible point. The fatal age in Mrs. Brett's hands was--not past, no, for here SHE was. But she might have died when she was twenty-one. Twenty-three seemed to be the utmost span. She was twenty-four, you know.

"I have said that I am a weak man. And you will have good proof of that directly. Yet I showed a certain amount of strength that day--yes, even on that day which has humiliated and saddened the rest of my life. Neither my face nor my voice betrayed me when in the palms of Dorothy Elbourn I was again confronted with those same signs. She was all for knowing the future, poor child! I believe I told her all manner of things that were to be. And she had no future--none, none in THIS world--except--

"And then, while I talked, there came to me suddenly a suspicion. I wondered it hadn't come before. You guess what it was? It made me feel very cold and strange. I went on talking. But, also, I went on--quite separately--thinking. The suspicion wasn't a certainty. This mother and daughter were always together. What was to befall the one might anywhere--anywhere--befall the other. But a like fate, in an equally near future, was in store for that other lady. The coincidence was curious, very. Here we all were together--here, they and I--I who was narrowly to escape, so soon now, what they, so soon now, were to suffer. Oh, there was an inference to be drawn. Not a sure inference, I told myself. And always I was talking, talking, and the train was swinging and swaying noisily along--to what? It was a fast train. Our carriage was near the engine. I was talking loudly. Full well I had known what I should see in the colonel's hands. I told myself I had not known. I told myself that even now the thing I dreaded was not sure to be. Don't think I was dreading it for myself. I wasn't so 'lamentable' as all that--now. It was only of them that I thought--only for them. I hurried over the colonel's character and career; I was perfunctory. It was Brett's hands that I wanted. THEY were the hands that mattered. If THEY had the marks-- Remember, Brett was to start for India in the coming week, his wife was to remain in England. They would be apart. Therefore--

"And the marks were there. And I did nothing--nothing but hold forth on the subtleties of Brett's character. There was a thing for me to do. I wanted to do it. I wanted to spring to the window and pull the communication-cord. Quite a simple thing to do. Nothing easier than to stop a train. You just give a sharp pull, and the train slows down, comes to a standstill. And the guard appears at your window.

You explain to the guard.

"Nothing easier than to tell him there is going to be a collision. Nothing easier than to insist that you and your friends and every other passenger in the train must get out at once. There ARE easier things than this? Things that need less courage than this? Some of THEM I could have done, I dare say. This thing I was going to do. Oh, I was determined that I would do it--directly.

"I had said all I had to say about Brett's hands. I had brought my entertainment to an end. I had been thanked and complimented all round. I was quite at liberty. I was going to do what I had to do. I was determined, yes.

"We were near the outskirts of London. The air was gray, thickening; and Dorothy Elbourn had said: 'Oh, this horrible old London! I suppose there's the same old fog!' And presently I heard her father saying something about 'prevention' and 'a short act of Parliament' and 'anthracite.' And I sat and listened and agreed and--"

Laider closed his eyes. He passed his hand slowly through the air.

"I had a racking headache. And when I said so, I was told not to talk. I was in bed, and the nurses were always telling me not to talk. I was in a hospital. I knew that; but I didn't know why I was there. One day I thought I should like to know why, and so I asked. I was feeling much better now. They told me by degrees that I had had concussion of the brain. I had been brought there unconscious, and had remained unconscious for forty-eight hours. I had been in an accident--a railway-accident. This seemed to me odd. I had arrived quite safely at my uncle's place, and I had no memory of any journey since that. In cases of concussion, you know, it's not uncommon for the patient to forget all that happened just before the accident; there may be a blank for several hours. So it was in my case. One day my uncle was allowed to come and see me. And somehow, suddenly, at sight of him, the blank was filled in. I remembered, in a flash, everything. I was quite calm, though. Or I made myself seem so, for I wanted to know how the collision had happened. My uncle told me that the engine-driver had failed to see a signal because of the fog, and our train had crashed into a goods-train.

"I didn't ask him about the people who were with me. You see, there was no need to ask.

"Very gently my uncle began to tell me, but--I had begun to talk strangely, I suppose. I remember the frightened look of my uncle's face, and the nurse scolding him in whispers.

"After that, all a blur. It seems that I became very ill indeed, wasn't expected to live.

"However, I live."

There was a long silence. Laider did not look at me, nor I at him. The fire was burning low, and he watched it.

At length he spoke:

"You despise me. Naturally. I despise myself."

"No, I don't despise you; but--"

"You blame me." I did not meet his gaze. "You blame me," he repeated.

"Yes."

"And there, if I may say so, you are a little unjust. It isn't my fault that I was born weak."

"But a man may conquer his weakness."

"Yes, if he is endowed with the strength for that."

His fatalism drew from me a gesture of disgust.

"Do you really mean," I asked, "that because you didn't pull that cord, you COULDN'T have pulled it?"

"Yes."

"And it's written in your hands that you couldn't?"

He looked at the palms of his hands.

"They are the hands of a very weak man," he said.

"A man so weak that he cannot believe in the possibility of free will for himself or for any one?"

"They are the hands of an intelligent man, who can weigh evidence and see things as they are."

"But answer me: Was it foreordained that you should not pull that cord?"

"It was foreordained."

"And was it actually marked in your hands that you were not going to pull it?"

"Ah, well, you see, it is rather the things one IS going to do that are actually marked. The things one isn't going to do,--the innumerable negative things,--how could one expect THEM to be marked?"

"But the consequences of what one leaves undone may be positive?"

"Horribly positive. My hand is the hand of a man who has suffered a great deal in later life."

"And was it the hand of a man DESTINED to suffer?"

"Oh, yes. I thought I told you that."

There was a pause.

"Well," I said, with awkward sympathy, "I suppose all hands are the hands of people destined to suffer."

"Not of people destined to suffer so much as _I_ have suffered--as I still suffer."

The insistence of his self-pity chilled me, and I harked back to a question he had not straightly answered.

"Tell me: Was it marked in your hands that you were not going to pull that cord?"

Again he looked at his hands, and then, having pressed them for a moment to his face, "It was marked very clearly," he answered, "in THEIR hands."

Two or three days after this colloquy there had occurred to me in London an idea--an ingenious and comfortable doubt. How was Laider to be sure that his brain, recovering from concussion, had REMEMBERED what happened in the course of that railway-journey? How was he to know that his brain hadn't simply, in its abeyance, INVENTED all this for him? It might be that he had never seen those signs in those hands. Assuredly, here was a bright loophole. I had forthwith written to Laider, pointing it out.

This was the letter which now, at my second visit, I had found miserably pent on the letter-board. I remembered my promise to rescue it. I arose from the retaining fireside, stretched my arms, yawned, and went forth to fulfil my Christian purpose. There was no one in the hall. The "shower" had at length ceased. The sun had positively come out, and the front door had been thrown open in its honor. Everything along the sea-front was beautifully gleaming, drying, shimmering. But I was not to be diverted from my purpose. I went to the letter-board. And--my letter was not there! Resourceful and plucky little thing--it had escaped! I did hope it would not be captured and brought back. Perhaps the alarm had already been raised by the tolling of that great bell which warns the inhabitants for miles around that a letter has broken loose from the letter-board. I had a vision of my envelop skimming wildly along the coast-line, pursued by the old, but active, waiter and a breathless pack of local worthies. I saw it outdistancing them all, dodging past coast-guards, doubling on its tracks, leaping breakwaters, unluckily injuring itself, losing speed, and at last, in a splendor of desperation, taking to the open sea. But suddenly I had another idea. Perhaps Laider had returned?

He had. I espied afar on the sands a form that was recognizably, by the listless droop of it, his. I was glad and sorry--rather glad, because he completed the scene of last year; and very sorry, because this time we should be at each other's mercy: no restful silence and liberty for either of us this time. Perhaps he had been told I was here, and had gone out to avoid me while he yet could. Oh weak, weak! Why palter? I put on my hat and coat, and marched out to meet him.

"Influenza, of course?" we asked simultaneously.

There is a limit to the time which one man may spend in talking to another about his own influenza; and presently, as we paced the sands, I felt that Laider had passed this limit. I wondered that he didn't break off and thank me now for my letter. He must have read it. He ought to have thanked me for it at once. It was a very good letter, a remarkable letter. But surely he wasn't waiting to answer it by post? His silence about it gave me the absurd sense of having taken a liberty, confound him! He was evidently ill at ease while he talked. But it wasn't for me to help him out of his difficulty, whatever that might be. It was for him to remove the strain imposed on myself.

Abruptly, after a long pause, he did now manage to say:

"It was--very good of you to--to write me that letter." He told me he had only just got it, and he drifted away into otiose explanations of this fact. I thought he might at least say it was a remarkable letter; and you can imagine my annoyance when he said, after another interval, "I was very much touched indeed." I had wished to be convincing, not touching. I can't bear to be called touching.

"Don't you," I asked, "think it IS quite possible that your brain invented all those memories of what--what happened before that accident?"

He drew a sharp sigh.

"You make me feel very guilty."

"That's exactly what I tried to make you NOT feel!"

"I know, yes. That's why I feel so guilty."

We had paused in our walk. He stood nervously prodding the hard wet sand with his walking-stick.

"In a way," he said, "your theory was quite right. But--it didn't go far enough. It's not only possible, it's a fact, that I didn't see those signs in those hands. I never examined those hands. They weren't there. _I_ wasn't there. I haven't an uncle in Hampshire, even. I never had."

I, too, prodded the sand.

"Well," I said at length, "I do feel rather a fool."

"I've no right even to beg your pardon, but--"

"Oh, I'm not vexed. Only--I rather wish you hadn't told me this."

"I wish I hadn't had to. It was your kindness, you see, that forced me. By trying to take an imaginary load off my conscience, you laid a very real one on it."

"I'm sorry. But you, of your own free will, you know, exposed your conscience to me last year. I don't yet quite understand why you did that."

"No, of course not. I don't deserve that you should. But I think you will. May I explain? I'm afraid I've talked a great deal already about my influenza, and I sha'n't be able to keep it out of my explanation. Well, my weakest point--I told you this last year, but it happens to be perfectly true that my weakest point--is my will. Influenza, as you know, fastens unerringly on one's weakest point. It doesn't attempt to undermine my imagination. That would be a forlorn hope. I have, alas! a very strong imagination. At ordinary times my imagination allows itself to be governed by my will. My will keeps it in check by constant nagging. But when my will isn't strong enough even to nag, then my imagination stampedes. I become even as a little child. I tell myself the most preposterous fables, and--the trouble is--I can't help telling them to my friends. Until I've thoroughly shaken off influenza, I'm not fit company for any one. I perfectly realize this, and I have the good sense to go right away till I'm quite well again. I come here usually. It seems absurd, but I must confess I was sorry last year when we fell into conversation. I knew I should very soon be letting myself go, or, rather, very soon be swept away. Perhaps I ought to have warned you; but--I'm a rather shy man. And then you mentioned the subject of palmistry. You said you believed in it. I wondered at that. I had once read Desbarolles's book about it, but I am bound to say I thought the whole thing very great nonsense indeed."

"Then," I gasped, "it isn't even true that you believe in palmistry?"

"Oh, no. But I wasn't able to tell you that. You had begun by saying that you believed in palmistry, and then you proceeded to scoff at it. While you scoffed I saw myself as a man with a terribly good reason for NOT scoffing; and in a flash I saw the terribly good reason; I had the whole story--at least I had the broad outlines of it--clear before me."

"You hadn't ever thought of it before?" He shook his head. My eyes beamed. "The whole thing was a sheer improvisation?"

"Yes," said Laider, humbly, "I am as bad as all that. I don't say that all the details of the story I told you that evening were filled in at the very instant of its conception. I was filling them in while we talked about palmistry in general, and while I was waiting for the moment when the story would come in most effectively. And I've no doubt I added some extra touches in the course of the actual telling. Don't imagine that I took the slightest pleasure in deceiving you. It's only my will, not my conscience, that is weakened after influenza. I simply can't help telling what I've made up, and telling it to the best of my ability. But I'm thoroughly ashamed all the time."

"Not of your ability, surely?"

"Yes, of that, too," he said, with his sad smile. "I always feel that I'm not doing justice to my idea."

"You are too stern a critic, believe me."

"It is very kind of you to say that. You are very kind altogether. Had I known that you were so essentially a man of the world, in the best sense of that term, I shouldn't have so much dreaded seeing you just now and having to confess to you. But I'm not going to take advantage of your urbanity and your easy-going ways. I hope that some day we may meet somewhere when I haven't had influenza and am a not wholly undesirable acquaintance. As it is, I refuse to let you associate with me. I am an older man than you, and so I may without impertinence warn you against having anything to do with me."

I deprecated this advice, of course; but for a man of weakened will he showed great firmness.

"You," he said, "in your heart of hearts, don't want to have to walk and talk continually with a person who might at any moment try to bamboozle you with some ridiculous tale. And I, for my part, don't want to degrade myself by trying to bamboozle any one, especially one whom I have taught to see through me. Let the two talks we have had be as though they had not been. Let us bow to each other, as last year, but let that be all. Let us follow in all things the precedent of last year."

With a smile that was almost gay he turned on his heel, and moved away with a step that was almost brisk. I was a little disconcerted. But I was also more than a little glad. The restfulness of silence, the charm of liberty--these things were not, after all, forfeit. My heart thanked Laider for that; and throughout the week I loyally seconded him in the system he had laid down for us. All was as it had been last year. We did not smile to each other, we merely bowed, when we entered or left the dining-room or smoking-room, and when we met on the wide-spread sands or in that shop which had a small and faded but circulating library.

Once or twice in the course of the week it did occur to me that perhaps Laider had told the simple truth at our first interview and an ingenious lie at our second. I frowned at this possibility. The idea of any one wishing to be quit of ME was most distasteful. However, I was to find reassurance. On the last evening of my stay I suggested, in the small smoking-room, that he and I should, as sticklers for precedent, converse. We did so very pleasantly. And after a while I happened to say that I had seen this afternoon a great number of sea-gulls flying close to the shore.

"Sea-gulls?" said Laider, turning in his chair.

"Yes. And I don't think I had ever realized how extraordinarily beautiful they are when their wings catch the light."

Laider threw a quick glance at me and away from me.

"You think them beautiful?"

"Surely."

"Well, perhaps they are, yes; I suppose they are. But--I don't like seeing them. They always remind me of something--rather an awful thing--that once happened to me."

IT was a very awful thing indeed.

The Codes Of Hammurabi And Moses
W. W. Davies

QTY

The discovery of the Hammurabi Code is one of the greatest achievements of archaeology, and is of paramount interest, not only to the student of the Bible, but also to all those interested in ancient history...

Religion   ISBN: *1-59462-338-4*   **Pages:132**
MSRP $12.95

The Theory of Moral Sentiments
Adam Smith

QTY

This work from 1749. contains original theories of conscience amd moral judgment and it is the foundation for systemof morals.

Philosophy ISBN: *1-59462-777-0*   **Pages:536**
MSRP $19.95

Jessica's First Prayer
Hesba Stretton

QTY

In a screened and secluded corner of one of the many railway-bridges which span the streets of London there could be seen a few years ago, from five o'clock every morning until half past eight, a tidily set-out coffee-stall, consisting of a trestle and board, upon which stood two large tin cans, with a small fire of charcoal burning under each so as to keep the coffee boiling during the early hours of the morning when the work-people were thronging into the city on their way to their daily toil...

Childrens   ISBN: *1-59462-373-2*   **Pages:84**
MSRP $9.95

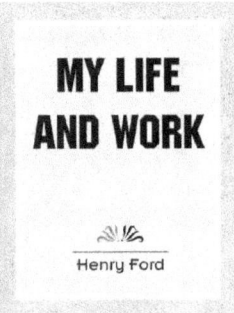

My Life and Work
Henry Ford

QTY

Henry Ford revolutionized the world with his implementation of mass production for the Model T automobile. Gain valuable business insight into his life and work with his own auto-biography... "We have only started on our development of our country we have not as yet, with all our talk of wonderful progress, done more than scratch the surface. The progress has been wonderful enough but..."

Biographies/   ISBN: *1-59462-198-5*   **Pages:300**
MSRP $21.95

The Art of Cross-Examination
Francis Wellman

QTY

I presume it is the experience of every author, after his first book is published upon an important subject, to be almost overwhelmed with a wealth of ideas and illustrations which could readily have been included in his book, and which to his own mind, at least, seem to make a second edition inevitable. Such certainly was the case with me; and when the first edition had reached its sixth impression in five months, I rejoiced to learn that it seemed to my publishers that the book had met with a sufficiently favorable reception to justify a second and considerably enlarged edition. ...

Pages:412

Reference   ISBN: *1-59462-647-2*   *MSRP $19.95*

On the Duty of Civil Disobedience
Henry David Thoreau

QTY

Thoreau wrote his famous essay, On the Duty of Civil Disobedience, as a protest against an unjust but popular war and the immoral but popular institution of slave-owning. He did more than write—he declined to pay his taxes, and was hauled off to gaol in consequence. Who can say how much this refusal of his hastened the end of the war and of slavery ?

Law   ISBN: *1-59462-747-9*   **Pages:48**

MSRP $7.45

Dream Psychology Psychoanalysis for Beginners
Sigmund Freud

QTY

Sigmund Freud, born Sigismund Schlomo Freud (May 6, 1856 - September 23, 1939), was a Jewish-Austrian neurologist and psychiatrist who co-founded the psychoanalytic school of psychology. Freud is best known for his theories of the unconscious mind, especially involving the mechanism of repression; his redefinition of sexual desire as mobile and directed towards a wide variety of objects; and his therapeutic techniques, especially his understanding of transference in the therapeutic relationship and the presumed value of dreams as sources of insight into unconscious desires.

Dream Psychology
Psychoanalysis for Beginners

Sigmund Freud

Pages:196

Psychology   ISBN: *1-59462-905-6*   *MSRP $15.45*

The Miracle of Right Thought
Orison Swett Marden

QTY

Believe with all of your heart that you will do what you were made to do. When the mind has once formed the habit of holding cheerful, happy, prosperous pictures, it will not be easy to form the opposite habit. It does not matter how improbable or how far away this realization may see, or how dark the prospects may be, if we visualize them as best we can, as vividly as possible, hold tenaciously to them and vigorously struggle to attain them, they will gradually become actualized, realized in the life. But a desire, a longing without endeavor, a yearning abandoned or held indifferently will vanish without realization.

Pages:360

Self Help   ISBN: *1-59462-644-8*   *MSRP $25.45*

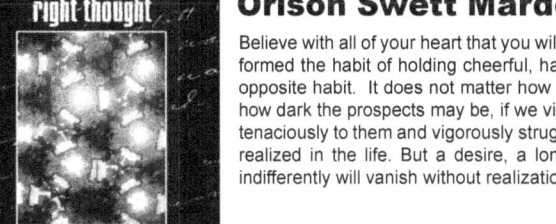

QTY

The Rosicrucian Cosmo-Conception Mystic Christianity *by Max Heindel*   ISBN: *1-59462-188-8*   **$38.95**
The Rosicrucian Cosmo-conception is not dogmatic, neither does it appeal to any other authority than the reason of the student. It is: not controversial, but is: sent forth in the, hope that it may help to clear...   *New Age/Religion Pages 646*

Abandonment To Divine Providence *by Jean-Pierre de Caussade*   ISBN: *1-59462-228-0*   **$25.95**
"The Rev. Jean Pierre de Caussade was one of the most remarkable spiritual writers of the Society of Jesus in France in the 18th Century. His death took place at Toulouse in 1751. His works have gone through many editions and have been republished...   *Inspirational/Religion Pages 400*

Mental Chemistry *by Charles Haanel*   ISBN: *1-59462-192-6*   **$23.95**
Mental Chemistry allows the change of material conditions by combining and appropriately utilizing the power of the mind. Much like applied chemistry creates something new and unique out of careful combinations of chemicals the mastery of mental chemistry...   *New Age Pages 354*

The Letters of Robert Browning and Elizabeth Barret Barrett 1845-1846 vol II   ISBN: *1-59462-193-4*   **$35.95**
by Robert Browning and Elizabeth Barrett   *Biographies Pages 596*

Gleanings In Genesis (volume I) *by Arthur W. Pink*   ISBN: *1-59462-130-6*   **$27.45**
Appropriately has Genesis been termed "the seed plot of the Bible" for in it we have, in germ form, almost all of the great doctrines which are afterwards fully developed in the books of Scripture which follow...   *Religion/Inspirational Pages 420*

The Master Key *by L. W. de Laurence*   ISBN: *1-59462-001-6*   **$30.95**
In no branch of human knowledge has there been a more lively increase of the spirit of research during the past few years than in the study of Psychology, Concentration and Mental Discipline. The requests for authentic lessons in Thought Control, Mental Discipline and...   *New Age/Business Pages 422*

The Lesser Key Of Solomon Goetia *by L. W. de Laurence*   ISBN: *1-59462-092-X*   **$9.95**
This translation of the first book of the "Lernegton" which is now for the first time made accessible to students of Talismanic Magic was done, after careful collation and edition, from numerous Ancient Manuscripts in Hebrew, Latin, and French...   *New Age/Occult Pages 92*

Rubaiyat Of Omar Khayyam *by Edward Fitzgerald*   ISBN:*1-59462-332-5*   **$13.95**
Edward Fitzgerald, whom the world has already learned, in spite of his own efforts to remain within the shadow of anonymity, to look upon as one of the rarest poets of the century, was born at Bredfield, in Suffolk, on the 31st of March, 1809. He was the third son of John Purcell...   *Music Pages 172*

Ancient Law *by Henry Maine*   ISBN: *1-59462-128-4*   **$29.95**
The chief object of the following pages is to indicate some of the earliest ideas of mankind, as they are reflected in Ancient Law, and to point out the relation of those ideas to modern thought.   *Religiom/History Pages 452*

Far-Away Stories *by William J. Locke*   ISBN: *1-59462-129-2*   **$19.45**
"Good wine needs no bush, but a collection of mixed vintages does. And this book is just such a collection. Some of the stories I do not want to remain buried for ever in the museum files of dead magazine-numbers an author's not unpardonable vanity..."   *Fiction Pages 272*

Life of David Crockett *by David Crockett*   ISBN: *1-59462-250-7*   **$27.45**
"Colonel David Crockett was one of the most remarkable men of the times in which he lived. Born in humble life, but gifted with a strong will, an indomitable courage, and unremitting perseverance...   *Biographies/New Age Pages 424*

Lip-Reading *by Edward Nitchie*   ISBN: *1-59462-206-X*   **$25.95**
Edward B. Nitchie, founder of the New York School for the Hard of Hearing, now the Nitchie School of Lip-Reading, Inc, wrote "LIP-READING Principles and Practice". The development and perfecting of this meritorious work on lip-reading was an undertaking...   *How-to Pages 400*

A Handbook of Suggestive Therapeutics, Applied Hypnotism, Psychic Science   ISBN: *1-59462-214-0*   **$24.95**
by Henry Munro   *Health/New Age/Health/Self-help Pages 376*

A Doll's House: and Two Other Plays *by Henrik Ibsen*   ISBN: *1-59462-112-8*   **$19.95**
Henrik Ibsen created this classic when in revolutionary 1848 Rome. Introducing some striking concepts in playwriting for the realist genre, this play has been studied the world over.   *Fiction/Classics/Plays 308*

The Light of Asia *by sir Edwin Arnold*   ISBN: *1-59462-204-3*   **$13.95**
In this poetic masterpiece, Edwin Arnold describes the life and teachings of Buddha. The man who was to become known as Buddha to the world was born as Prince Gautama of India but he rejected the worldly riches and abandoned the reigns of power when...   *Religion/History/Biographies Pages 170*

The Complete Works of Guy de Maupassant *by Guy de Maupassant*   ISBN: *1-59462-157-8*   **$16.95**
"For days and days, nights and nights, I had dreamed of that first kiss which was to consecrate our engagement, and I knew not on what spot I should put my lips..."   *Fiction/Classics Pages 240*

The Art of Cross-Examination *by Francis L. Wellman*   ISBN: *1-59462-309-5*   **$26.95**
Written by a renowned trial lawyer, Wellman imparts his experience and uses case studies to explain how to use psychology to extract desired information through questioning.   *How-to/Science/Reference Pages 408*

Answered or Unanswered? *by Louisa Vaughan*   ISBN: *1-59462-248-5*   **$10.95**
Miracles of Faith in China   *Religion Pages 112*

The Edinburgh Lectures on Mental Science (1909) *by Thomas*   ISBN: *1-59462-008-3*   **$11.95**
This book contains the substance of a course of lectures recently given by the writer in the Queen Street Hall, Edinburgh. Its purpose is to indicate the Natural Principles governing the relation between Mental Action and Material Conditions...   *New Age/Psychology Pages 148*

Ayesha *by H. Rider Haggard*   ISBN: *1-59462-301-5*   **$24.95**
Verily and indeed it is the unexpected that happens! Probably if there was one person upon the earth from whom the Editor of this, and of a certain previous history, did not expect to hear again...   *Classics Pages 380*

Ayala's Angel *by Anthony Trollope*   ISBN: *1-59462-352-X*   **$29.95**
The two girls were both pretty, but Lucy who was twenty-one who supposed to be simple and comparatively unattractive, whereas Ayala was credited, as her Bombwhat romantic name might show, with poetic charm and a taste for romance. Ayala when her father died was nineteen...   *Fiction Pages 484*

The American Commonwealth *by James Bryce*   ISBN: *1-59462-286-8*   **$34.45**
An interpretation of American democratic political theory. It examines political mechanics and society from the perspective of Scotsman James Bryce   *Politics Pages 572*

Stories of the Pilgrims *by Margaret P. Pumphrey*   ISBN: *1-59462-116-0*   **$17.95**
This book explores pilgrims religious oppression in England as well as their escape to Holland and eventual crossing to America on the Mayflower, and their early days in New England...   *History Pages 268*

QTY

The Fasting Cure *by Sinclair Upton* ISBN: *1-59462-222-1* **$13.95**
In the Cosmopolitan Magazine for May, 1910, and in the Contemporary Review (London) for April, 1910, I published an article dealing with my experiences in fasting. I have written a great many magazine articles, but never one which attracted so much attention... New Age/Self Help/Health Pages 164

Hebrew Astrology *by Sepharial* ISBN: *1-59462-308-2* **$13.45**
In these days of advanced thinking it is a matter of common observation that we have left many of the old landmarks behind and that we are now pressing forward to greater heights and to a wider horizon than that which represented the mind-content of our progenitors... Astrology Pages 144

Thought Vibration or The Law of Attraction in the Thought World ISBN: *1-59462-127-6* **$12.95**
by William Walker Atkinson *Psychology/Religion Pages 144*

Optimism *by Helen Keller* ISBN: *1-59462-108-X* **$15.95**
Helen Keller was blind, deaf, and mute since 19 months old, yet famously learned how to overcome these handicaps, communicate with the world, and spread her lectures promoting optimism. An inspiring read for everyone... Biographies/Inspirational Pages 84

Sara Crewe *by Frances Burnett* ISBN: *1-59462-360-0* **$9.45**
In the first place, Miss Minchin lived in London. Her home was a large, dull, tall one, in a large, dull square, where all the houses were alike, and all the sparrows were alike, and where all the door-knockers made the same heavy sound... Childrens/Classic Pages 88

The Autobiography of Benjamin Franklin *by Benjamin Franklin* ISBN: *1-59462-135-7* **$24.95**
The Autobiography of Benjamin Franklin has probably been more extensively read than any other American historical work, and no other book of its kind has had such ups and downs of fortune. Franklin lived for many years in England, where he was agent... Biographies/History Pages 332

Name	
Email	
Telephone	
Address	
City, State ZIP	

☐ **Credit Card** ☐ **Check / Money Order**

Credit Card Number	
Expiration Date	
Signature	

Please Mail to: Book Jungle
PO Box 2226
Champaign, IL 61825
or Fax to: 630-214-0564

ORDERING INFORMATION

web*: www.bookjungle.com*
email*: sales@bookjungle.com*
fax*: 630-214-0564*
mail*: Book Jungle PO Box 2226 Champaign, IL 61825*
or PayPal *to sales@bookjungle.com*

Please contact us for bulk discounts

DIRECT-ORDER TERMS

20% Discount if You Order
Two or More Books
Free Domestic Shipping!
Accepted: Master Card, Visa,
Discover, American Express